Lost
at the
Mall

With love
to
Tony and Alison

Library of Congress Cataloging in Publication Data

Fryar, Jane L., 1950–
      Lost at the mall: featuring Morris the mouse / Jane L. Fryar: illustrated by Deborah G. Wilson.
      Summary: Morris the mouse reminds his human friend to pray when he becomes lost in a shopping mall.
      ISBN 0-570-04196-1
      [1. Lost children—Fiction. 2. Shopping malls—Fiction. 3. Mice—Fiction. 4. Christian life—Fiction.] I. Deborah G. Wilson, ill. II. Title.
PZ7.F92535Lp   1991
[E]—dc20   90-47447
                                                                                                   CIP
                                                                                                    AC

1   2   3   4   5   6   7   8   9   10   99   98   97   96   95   94   93   92   91

Lost
at the
Mall

Featuring
Morris the Mouse

Jane L. Fryar

Illustrated by
Deborah G. Wilson

Publishing House
St. Louis

Morris wriggled with excitement deep inside Broderick's big parka pocket. Morris had never visited a shopping mall before. Now he was on his way!

Broderick and Morris are special friends. Morris lives secretly in Broderick's Sunday school classroom. No one except Broderick knows about Morris. No one else has ever seen him. Not even Mrs. Marshall, Broderick's Sunday school teacher.

This morning, after Sunday school, Broderick sneaked back to his classroom. He helped Morris slip into his deep, dark parka pocket. And away they went.

Bump. Bump. Bump. Morris bumped up and down as Broderick skipped down the long church hallway.

Varoom. Varoom. Varoom. Broderick and Daddy drove to the big shopping mall after church.

"Hold on tight to my hand," said Daddy. "Lots of people are shopping today. Let's stick together, okay?"

"Okay, Daddy," said Broderick.

Morris peeked out from Broderick's parka pocket. All the colors!
All the people! All the music and noise!
"Wow!" whispered Morris.

Daddy and Broderick walked and walked in the mall.
Walk.

Walk.

Walk.

Bump,

bump,

bump,

went Morris.

Then Daddy stopped to look at something. He talked to a sales clerk.
Stand.

Stand.

Stand.

Broderick felt hot inside his big, bright parka.
Morris felt hot inside Broderick's parka pocket. He poked his
head out.

"Psst!" whispered Morris. "Look at that!"

Scitter.

Scatter.

Hop!

The mechanical mouse danced and danced.
"Tee-hee, hee, hee . . . "
Morris and Broderick giggled and giggled. Morris had never seen
a mechanical mouse before.
"Wait 'til I tell my big brother, Maynard," said Morris.

Suddenly Morris looked up.

"Oh," he said. Broderick looked at Morris. Then he looked up at Daddy. But Daddy wasn't there!

"Oh!" said Broderick. "Oh, no!"

"Where's Daddy?" said Broderick in a very small voice.
"I can't see him anywhere."
Morris looked this way and that.
Broderick looked that way and this.
But Daddy was nowhere in sight.

After a long time, Broderick sat down.
"Oh, Morris," said Broderick. "I feel scared."

"Daddy said I should hold on tight, Morris. But I didn't. Now he's lost. And I'm lost, too. What will I do?"

"Well . . . " said Morris slowly. "I have an idea. You could ask Jesus to help you find your daddy, couldn't you?"

"Nope," sighed Broderick. "I should have listened to Daddy, Morris. But I didn't. I can't ask Jesus to help me now."

"Sure you could!" said Morris. "Sure you could! Mrs. Marshall said so in Sunday school today!"

"Just look at that paper she gave you. It went crinkle, crinkle, crinkle inside your pocket whenever I went bump, bump, bump."

"I listened from my front door," said Morris. " I always listen because I like to hear all the children sing their happy songs to Jesus."

Broderick smiled and wiped away a tear.

"I heard Mrs. Marshall say that Jesus died to forgive boys and girls," said Morris. "She said that, didn't she, Broderick? Didn't she say that Jesus always, always loves and forgives you?"

"Yes," sniffed Broderick. "That's what she said."

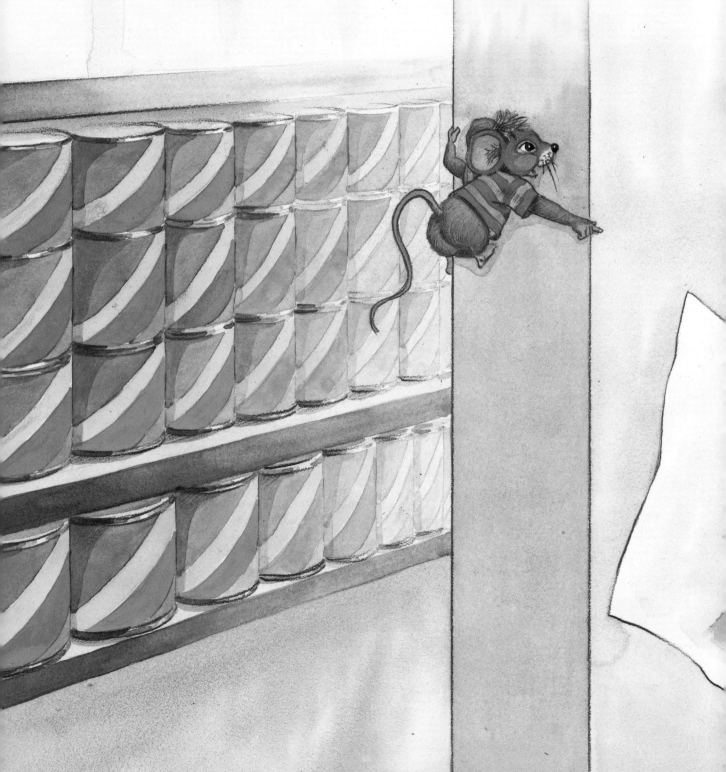

"Well," said Morris. "Do you think you could ask Jesus to help you?"

Broderick thought for a minute. Then he sniffed a quiet, "Yes." And that's just what Broderick did.

"Dear Jesus," he prayed. "I'm sorry that I didn't keep close to Daddy like he said. Please forgive me. And help me find him. Please. Amen."

Squeak. Squeak. Squeak.

"Oh," squealed Morris. "I know *that* squeak!" He leaped back into Broderick's parka pocket.

"Why, Broderick!" said a familiar voice. "Whatever are you doing here?"

"Oh, Mrs. Marshall," said Broderick. "I'm lost. Did Jesus send you to help me find my Daddy?"

"Well, here I am," said Mrs. Marshall, "so I guess He did!"
And off they went to look.

About Your Child

"Well . . ." said Morris slowly. "I have an idea. You could ask Jesus to help you find your daddy, couldn't you?" "Nope," sighed Broderick. "I should have listened to Daddy, Morris. But I didn't. I can't ask Jesus to help me now."

The wonder of God's forgiveness. His unchanging willingness to help us. All of us find ourselves doubting these truths sometimes—especially when the messes we face are of our own making.

Did Jesus hear Broderick's prayer? Did Jesus forgive Broderick? Did Jesus help Broderick even though Broderick had disobeyed Daddy?

Yes. Yes. And yes.

Your child will probably be able to answer these questions correctly. But the true test will come in the days and weeks ahead. Talk together about God's love and forgiveness often, especially when your child struggles with a problem brought about by his or her own wrong-doing. Gently lead your child to see both the sin and the trouble that sin has caused.

Listen as your child asks our heavenly Father's forgiveness. Together, remember that God promises to forgive us for Jesus' sake.

Jane L. Fryar